Walking through a World of Aromas

Text © 2012 Ariel Andrés Almada
Illustrations © 2012 Sonja Wimmer
This edition © 2012 Cuento de Luz SL
Calle Claveles 10 | Urb Monteclaro | Pozuelo de Alarcón | 28223 Madrid | Spain
www.cuentodeluz.com
Original title in Spanish: La niña que caminaba entre aromas
English translation by Jon Brokenbrow
ISBN: 978-84-15619-48-2
Printed by Shanghai Chenxi Printing Co., Ltd. in PRC, August 2012, print number 1305-01

To our dog Tomi, who has given us so much

love for so many years ...

— Ariel Andrés Almada

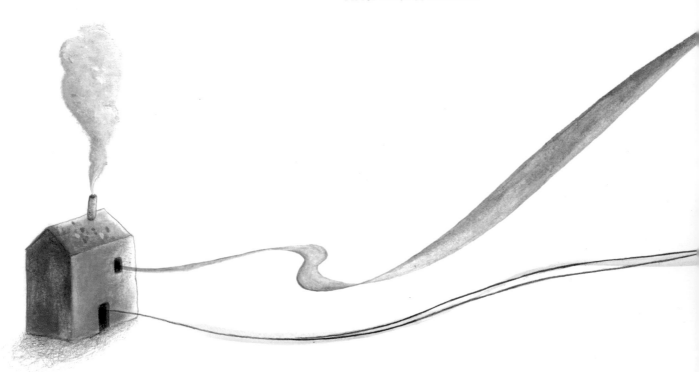

CUENTO
DE LUZ

Walking through a World of AROMAS

Ariel Andrés Almada & Sonja Wimmer

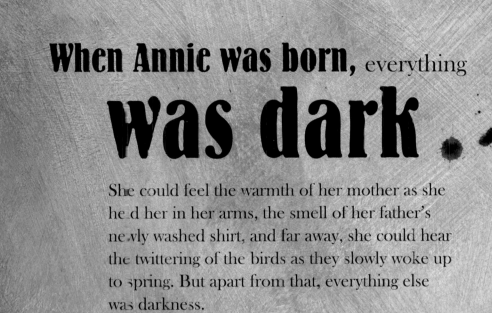

When Annie was born, everything was dark.

She could feel the warmth of her mother as she held her in her arms, the smell of her father's newly washed shirt, and far away, she could hear the twittering of the birds as they slowly woke up to spring. But apart from that, everything else was darkness.

As the years went by, Annie understood that she was different. She heard her friends talking about colors and shapes, but everything was confusing for her. One day, her mother said to her:

"Blue
feels like this,"

and made her hold an ice
cube in her hands.

"And **red** feels like this,"

while she made her hold out her hands towards the fireplace, very carefully so as not to burn them. Annie smiled and turned her head in the direction of her mother's voice.

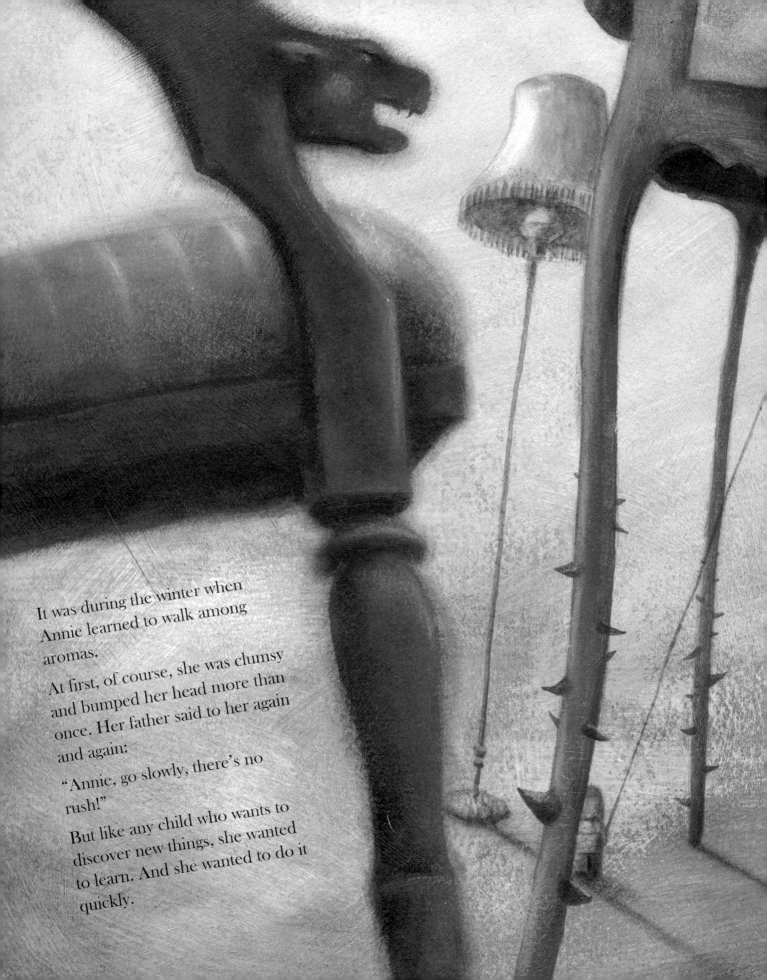

It was during the winter when Annie learned to walk among aromas.

At first, of course, she was clumsy and bumped her head more than once. Her father said to her again and again:

"Annie, go slowly, there's no rush!"

But like any child who wants to discover new things, she wanted to learn. And she wanted to do it quickly.

So one day, she began to dodge the old furniture in her house. She knew that it was polished with wax that had a very special smell, which she could easily detect. If she walked close to it, the smell became stronger, gradually disappearing as she moved away. One step this way, one step that way, and the dining room table was behind her. One step to the left, three to the right, and she could dance all the way from the kitchen to her room without any help. The next week she learned to walk next to the vases full of newly cut roses, to reach the kitchen guided by the smell of fresh-baked cookies that her grandma made, and even not to step on the tail of her pet cat, Paris, who for some funny reason always smelled of cinnamon.

And then one day, and without knowing exactly how, Annie realized that although she was different, she could do very special things.

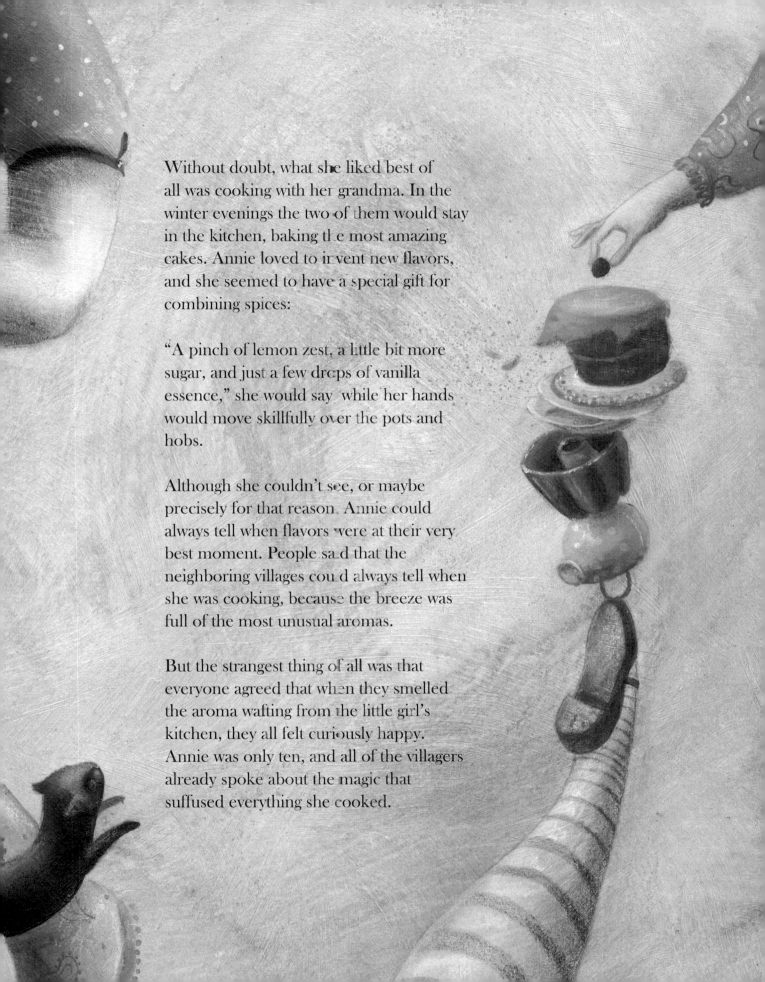

Without doubt, what she liked best of all was cooking with her grandma. In the winter evenings the two of them would stay in the kitchen, baking the most amazing cakes. Annie loved to invent new flavors, and she seemed to have a special gift for combining spices:

"A pinch of lemon zest, a little bit more sugar, and just a few drops of vanilla essence," she would say while her hands would move skillfully over the pots and hobs.

Although she couldn't see, or maybe precisely for that reason, Annie could always tell when flavors were at their very best moment. People said that the neighboring villages could always tell when she was cooking, because the breeze was full of the most unusual aromas.

But the strangest thing of all was that everyone agreed that when they smelled the aroma wafting from the little girl's kitchen, they all felt curiously happy. Annie was only ten, and all of the villagers already spoke about the magic that suffused everything she cooked.

The summers and falls went by, and the winters and springs, and then the summers would come again while Annie continued to experiment with the flavors and spices that her father would bring to her from the most far-away places. On her seventeenth birthday, Annie surprised her family with a very special dinner. A few days earlier, she had asked each of them to tell her which was the happiest moment of their lives. Her mother had told her it was when she was born. Her father said it was when he first visited the village where they now lived, and her grandma said it was when her husband had proposed to her on a night when it was raining cats and dogs.

On the night of the dinner, Annie brought out plates with different dishes for each of them. Next, she blindfolded them and whispered to them to start eating. At first they didn't notice anything strange, except that the food smelled quite marvelous. Her grandma was the first one to realize. She couldn't explain how or why, but she was suddenly transported to the same place on the same rainy night at precisely the same moment that she said "Yes, I will" to the man who would be her husband for so many years. While she struggled with shaking hands to take another bite, she realized that she wasn't the only one who was crying. Annie's mother and father, each one lost in their own memories, were chewing with tears running down their cheeks. When the dinner was over, they all hugged Annie, and she didn't need to see them to feel the gratitude in their hearts.

The news spread like wildfire among the villagers. Annie had the gift of being able to awaken the strangest emotions with her magical mixtures of spices. One day, Mrs. Mittrel asked her to bake some cookies for her husband, who had laid in bed for several days and did not have the energy to

get up. Mr. Jonas asked her to make a cake for his son, who was feeling terrible because he could not pass his exams, and even the mayor of a nearby town wrote to Annie, asking her to send him something that would cheer up his mother, who was filled with sorrow. Annie loved knowing that she was helping others while she did what she liked best: cooking. Although she never accepted money, her neighbors made sure she was never short of anything. The local carpenter made her wooden spoons, which Annie loved for their smooth feel, and all of the others always gave her special presents. Her life was tranquil, her days spent surrounded by aromas and the warmth of the oven.

Despite her skills, there was one person Annie didn't seem to be able to help. Julian had been born in the same hospital as her, just a few minutes earlier, and their cries rang through the air together on that day. But apart from that, they had never met again. One day, the young man who spent his time going on long, slow

orangeblossom

azafrán saffron

walks was convinced by his mother to visit the amazing cook. His mother insisted that only she could help him to overcome the lethargy that had afflicted him for years. Julian wasn't too sure that a few recipes were going to help him, but finally he decided to go visit Annie.

The very first time he set eyes on her, all
he could think of was spending the rest of
his life counting the freckles on her
cheeks. Annie was already a beautiful
young woman, with auburn hair and a
sparkling smile. Julian's legs shook as
he began to tell her about his problem
while she mixed orange essence with half
a spoon of jasmine honey and a pinch
of saffron. Then she took a brush and
spread the mixture over some recently
baked cookies, wrapped them in a white
cloth and gave them to Julian, reminding
him to eat one every morning when he
woke up and another before he went to
sleep. Julian thanked her, and promised
that he would tell her if there was any
change.

But the days went by, turning into weeks and months, without Julian showing any signs of improvement. Annie had tried all of the possible combinations of spices, and had even asked her father to look for a particularly exotic type of pepper in India, which was said to make miracles happen. Every week Julian would return to Annie's house, and she knew it was him because she could hear his feet dragging along the ground from far, far away. Sometimes they would take long walks around the lake with green water next to the village, and would talk for hours about Julian's problems. Other times they would lay down in the grass while he told her what the stars looked like, and she would imagine millions and millions of suns scattered like grains of mustard on the table. Annie didn't know anything about shapes or colors, but in her imagination she had created the whole of his world, and she loved his voice as he described it to her.

Sometimes Julian would offer her his arm to guide her, but Annie would gracefully insist on walking on her own.

"If I hadn't met you, I never would have thought it possible that someone could get around being guided only by aromas," he said to her.

She smiled and said, "My mother said it was precisely for that reason, because I didn't know it was impossible, that I learned to do it."

Entering the kitchen one fall afternoon, Annie noticed the fragrance of her grandma, who sat waiting for her with a mischievous smile.

"Did you enjoy your walk with Julian?" asked the old lady.
Annie, without knowing why, suddenly felt herself blush.

"I can't find a way to help him," she answered, none too certainly.
"I've tried all of the recipes you've shown me, and all of the ones I've created myself. There's nothing left for me to try."

"You know something, Annie?" said her grandma. "Since you were a little girl, you've been able to see into other people's hearts. Maybe now it's time for you to start to look into your own, don't you think?"

It was then that Annie understood that Julian had overcome his sadness long, long ago, and it had nothing to do with the honey, or the cinnamon, or the vanilla or the saffron. But above all, she knew how sad she would feel if the day ever came when she didn't hear him dragging his feet along the path. She understood that for all this time he had been waiting for her—she who felt so secure treating other people's hearts with her recipes—to pluck up the courage to discover that true love, like all great dishes, takes a long time to prepare, and that, most of all, it needs patience. A great deal of patience.

Smiling, Annie turned to her grandma and said almost in a whisper, so as not to wake her cat, "I think I'll make something special for when Julian comes to visit me this afternoon. Can you pass me the sugar bowl?"